Thomas Buchanan Read, Lizbeth Bullock Humphrey

Drifting

Thomas Buchanan Read, Lizbeth Bullock Humphrey

Drifting

ISBN/EAN: 9783743604421

Printed in Europe, USA, Canada, Australia, Japan

Cover: Foto ©Andreas Hilbeck / pixelio.de

Manufactured and distributed by brebook publishing software
(www.brebook.com)

Thomas Buchanan Read, Lizbeth Bullock Humphrey

Drifting

DRIFTING.

BY

T. BUCHANAN READ.

. . . .

ILLUSTRATED

FROM DESIGNS BY MISS L. B. HUMPHREY.

. . . .

PHILADELPHIA

J. B. LIPPINCOTT COMPANY.

715 AND 717 MARKET STREET.

DRIFTING.

DRIFTING.

My soul to-day
    Is far away,
      Sailing the Vesuvian Bay;
  My wingéd boat,
  A bird afloat,
Swims round the purple peaks remote:—

ROUND purple peaks
　　　It sails, and seeks
Blue inlets and their crystal creeks,
　　Where high rocks throw,
　　Through deeps below,
A duplicated golden glow.

F̲A̲R̲, vague, and dim,
　　The mountains swim ;
While on Vesuvius' misty brim,
　　With outstretched hands,
　　The gray smoke stands
O'erlooking the volcanic lands.

IN lofty lines,
    'Mid palms and pines,
And olives, aloes, elms, and vines,
    Sorrento swings
    On sunset wings,
Where Tasso's spirit soars and sings.

HERE Ischia smiles
O'er liquid miles;
And yonder, bluest of the isles,
Calm Capri waits,
Her sapphire gates
Beguiling to her bright estates.

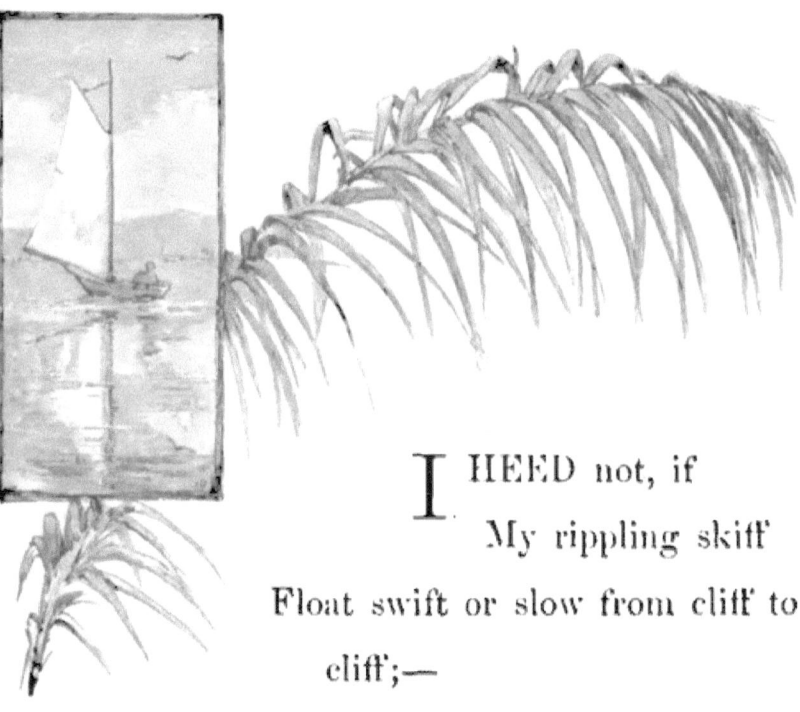

I HEED not, if
My rippling skiff
Float swift or slow from cliff to
cliff;—
With dreamful eyes
My spirit lies
Under the walls of Paradise.

Under the walls
Where swells and falls
The Bay's deep breast at intervals

At peace I lie,
Blown softly by,
A cloud upon this liquid sky.

The day, so mild,
Is Heaven's own child,
With Earth and Ocean reconciled;—
The airs I feel
Around me steal
Are murmuring to the murmuring keel.

OVER the rail
My hand I trail
Within the shadow of the sail,
A joy intense,
The cooling sense
Glides down my drowsy indolence

WITH dreamful eyes
My spirit lies
Where Summer sings and never
dies,—
O'erveiled with vines,
She glows and shines
Among her future oil and wines.

HER children, hid
   The cliffs amid,
Are gambolling with the
   gambolling kid;
Or down the walls,
With tipsy calls,
Laugh on the rocks like
   waterfalls.

THE fisher's child,
　　With tresses wild,
Unto the smooth, bright sand beguiled,
　　With glowing lips
　　Sings as she skips,
Or gazes at the far-off ships.

YON deep bark goes
Where Traffic blows,
From lands of sun to lands
of snows :—

This happier one,
Its course is run
From lands of snow to
lands of sun.

O HAPPY ship,
To rise and dip,
With the blue crystal at your lip!
O happy crew,
My heart with you
Sails, and sails, and sings anew!

No more, no more
  The worldly shore
Upbraids me with its loud uproar!
  With dreamful eyes
  My spirit lies
Under the walls of Paradise!

.